ANGELL'S ANIMALS

Wild Friends In An Urban World

by

Madeline Angell

Illustrated

by

Marie McNamara

Angell's Animals
Wild Friends in an Urban World

Published by Lone Oak Press, Ltd.
Red Wing, Minnesota

Printed in the United States of America

First Edition
ISBN 1-883477-45-X
Library of Congress CIP: 00-107887

Contents

CHOPPER

I would be willing to bet that not many people, if any, have seen a blanket flying through the air propelled by a great horned owl. I never expect to see it again, but my husband and younger son witnessed it also, and so I know it was not my imagination.

It all started when a very young great horned owl was taken from its nest by a young boy under the guidance of a self-proclaimed naturalist. The boy cared for it, and a few weeks later, took it to college with him. The owl was named by the boy and his roommates "Chopper" because, not knowing how to hoot, he expressed his emotions with a chop-chop sound. An alternate sound he made was a squawk like that of a very large, hungry baby robin.

For various reasons Chopper did not prove to be a very desirable roommate in a college

dormitory, so the boy left the owl at his home, which was about fifty miles away. For somewhat the same reasons, the boy's mother did not appreciate having Chopper as a house guest. She took him outdoors and turned him loose.

At this point, Chopper was unable to fly, and he was starving, due to the fact that he had not had his parents to teach him how to hunt to food. Desperate, he crossed a busy street, hopped through some yards, climbed a hill and arrived in our yard.

Chopper's first relationship with our family was with Mac, our much beloved Scotty. It so happened that my husband and I were gone for the day. Randy's older brother was away at college. Randy put Mac out in the side yard, which terminated in a steep, wooded hill, and snapped the clasp of his rope to his collar. (The two times Mac, who also had a fenced in back yard, got loose, he was unable to find his way home.) Randy then went back in the house for his breakfast. He heard a bang against the side of the house, followed by a commotion in the yard. Mac was barking at something with great excitement.

Hurrying outdoors, Randy stared, hardly able to believe his eyes. The object of Mac's yaps

was a big horned owl with wings arched aggressively and feathers puffed out so that he looked bigger than the dog and twice as tough. Mac, incidentally was an angelic tempered pooch who barked ferociously at mailmen, grocery boys and paper boys, but had such a deficiency of killer instinct that he could play with a box elder bug ten minutes or so without injuring it. In spite of his fierce bark, the only times Mac ever came close to violence were times when another dog tried to start a fight. On those occasions Mac just stood his ground and looked rather shocked about the whole idea. Since he was always rescued immediately from such potentially unpleasant situations, Mac had led a rather sheltered life.

The owl was clacking his beak. With his ear tufts standing straight up, his face looked more like that of a cat than a bird.

Curiously enough, the owl seemed to believe he could hold both Mac and Randy at bay. He made no effort to retreat. What went on between Mac and the owl before Randy arrived is a matter of conjecture. Mac must have been more curious than frightened, since he was later discovered to have a couple of owl feathers on his nose. There is, of course, the possibility that he sniffed the feathers up from the sidewalk where the owl had been; however, we gave him the benefit of the doubt and concluded that he actually had touched the fearsome bird with his nose.

At any rate, when Randy came out of the house, Mac was only a couple of inches from the bird and was barking his very fiercest. The general direction of his leaning, however,. was backwards, until he felt the security of Randy's hand on his rope. Then he had to be restrained from leaping forward by Randy's pull against the rope, and once in the house he sat up and begged to go outdoors again.

Randy was worried about the possibility that the owl was sick, perhaps even had rabies, and that the owl might have transmitted the disease to the dog. A normal, healthy owl certainly would not behave as this owl was behaving.

When Mac was safely in the house, Randy inspected him, but could not see that the owl had done the dog any damage. Randy must have looked rather unfriendly to the owl, for the owl hopped across the lawn, spreading his wings now and then to assist his progress. The yard was quite large, with a tall lilac hedge separating it from the wooded hill, at the bottom of which was a residential district. The owl waddled awkwardly through the opening in the hedge. Randy followed him, and discovered that the bird had managed to get on top of an abandoned picnic table on the other side of the hedge. The bird squawked at Randy and clacked his bill at him. "Chop, chop, chop, squaaawk!" he said.

Although he was intrigued by the owl, Randy could not loiter for further observation, since it was time for him to start down the hill toward school. On his way back to the kitchen to finish his now-soggy Cornflakes and get his schoolbooks, Randy observed a bloody patch on the side of the house, near the spot where he had first seen the owl. That explained the bumping sound which had first captured Randy's attention. The owl must have banged against the side of the house, and might have been slightly injured.

Although there was no time for Randy to do anything about the situation, other than give the bloodstain a brief squirt with the hose, he knew someone who did have the time. He called his grandparents, who lived a short distance away, and reported the morning's activities. Grandpa Ben said he would come over and take look at the owl to see what could be done.

Grandpa Ben arrived a short time later with some hamburger and a small aluminum dish for holding water. Grandpa, a bird and animal lover since childhood, soft-talked his way close to the owl and stretched out his hand with an offering of hamburger. He placed the meat near the owl and went to fill the water dish from the hose. When he returned the hamburger was gone, and the owl was up on a low branch of the oak tree which overspread the picnic table. Grandpa Ben coaxed the bird to come for water, but although the owl regarded him fixedly with his bright golden eyes, and rocked back and forth in excitement, he would not come. Grandpa left the water on the table where the bird could drink it if he so desired. He returned later in the day, but saw no sign of the big bird. Nor did Randy, when he returned from school. He called the veterinarian and was assured that owls were not subject to rabies.

When we returned home that night, there was much talk about the owl who apparently could not fly and who did not seem to be afraid of people.

The next morning was warm enough so that I had the windows open as I went about the chores of making beds and sorting out the laundry. A now-and-then wind swirled the fallen leaves, yellow and brown, picked them up, circled them, and dropped them again. It gently tugged at dry leaves still clinging to branches, caught some of them in its grasp and carried them playfully to the ground. I closed my eyes and savored a deep breath full of the sweet-sad scent of crispy autumn, and as I did so I heard a peculiar sound.

It was a sound difficult to describe. For lack of a better term, I will call it a squawk, and on this particular occasion, there was a note of great distress to the squawk, since the sound was coming from an owl that was starving to death. He also made a chop-chop sound by snapping his beak.

Never one to put work ahead of satisfying curiosity, I slipped on a sweater and went outdoors to seek the source of this strange noise. Following the sound, I went through the hedge and into the woods and came face-to-face with the creature who emitted these squawks at rhythmic intervals. I recognized it at once as the creature who had been in our yard the day before.

A fallen tree was resting at a forty-five degree angle to the ground; three fourths of the way up the trunk of this tree was the bird that was calling out in distress. It was the biggest owl I had ever seen, and since I had been a bird-watcher for years, I knew this was a great horned owl. Anyone who has had much to do with birds or animals knows they have a way of communicating their mood and desires to receptive humans. This owl was definitely calling for help. The tone of his call, the pleading look in his blazing yellow eyes told me this. But how could I feed him? My dad had fed him hamburger, but this was when the owl was sitting on the picnic table. How was I to get meat up to where the bird was now sitting? I didn't care for the idea of holding it out in my hand. I might end up minus a finger or two.

I made several attempts to feed him that day. Rolling up chunks of hamburger, I placed them on the dead branch where he sat. He looked at them with interest, but made no attempt to retrieve them. He continued to communicate with me in his excited fashion. At one point he did a peculiar thing. Between the two of us was a tall weed blocking our vision of one another. I was very aware of this because I was thinking of taking a picture of him, and this weed would interfere. Suddenly the owl, after peering on one side of the weed and the other, reached over and snapped it in two with his beak. He still did not eat the meat and so I left. Later in the day the meat was gone.

What happened the next morning must have amused any neighbors who happened to be watching. I heard the owl calling from across the road. I was still in my housecoat, but I did not want the starving owl to give up hope of being fed, so I grabbed a small hunk of hamburger and crossed the road. I saw him on the ground, very excited, as indicated by his clicking of the beak and his swaying from side to side. I held out the piece of meat and he began to hop toward me. He had nearly reached me when I suddenly became afraid. What if he should attack me? I knew that great horned owls were described by some authorities as "untamably ferocious". I tossed the meat in his direction, gathered up my long skirt, and ran for the house. The owl followed me part way, right at my heels. In my cowardliness I cried out "No! No!"

When I realized the bird was no longer following me, I stopped and looked back at him. I felt ashamed of myself and spoke gently to him before returning to the house for more food. He missed the first chunk I tossed to him.

When I returned to throw him another ball of hamburger he pounced on it, held it firmly in place with his enormous talons and gulped it hungrily. His excited squawk diminished to a higher, softer , gurgling sound. In fact, he was so busy expressing pleasure that a couple of times he nearly choked on his food. The second piece he also ate. Then he retreated to the woods. He still squawked, but there was a different tone to his call now. It had overtones of contentment.

Gradually the feeling of trust between the big bird and me increased. He now came to a shelf on the big oak closest to the kitchen (more about the shelf in connection with the squirrels). He waited there for me to feed him. By this time we had learned about his background and the fact that he had been named Chopper, and so that is what we now called him.

Chopper quickly became famous in our neighborhood. Although he would not come to me for feeding when spectators were watching, he often talked to them with his "chop-chop" conversation. I became known as the "owl lady".

Our family did agree that Chopper would be better off in the Mississippi bottomlands near the area which had been his original home, but we were not sure he could make it on his own, since owl youngsters are cared for by their parents for months.

So I wrote to the director of the Como Zoo in Saint Paul, Minnesota, which was fifty miles away. The director replied that the zoo had no money at present to come and get the owl. He warned that I should have as little to do with him as possible because of his razor-sharp talons. I took reasonable precautions, but was not about to abandon this great-horned owl who had been deprived of his parents.

A crisis arose when three boys, about the age of the boy who had taken Chopper from his nest on the advice of a so-called naturalist, cut through our yard. Chopper had ridden on his young master's shoulder and apparently remembered this. He landed on the shoulder of one of the boys. The boy was terrified. He shouted and began to run. Chopper flew back to his favorite oak tree.

I did not learn about the incident until I received a call from the police department telling me that a big owl had attacked a boy in our yard, and that we must get rid of the bird.

As a result our family decided we would try to return Chopper to the bottomlands from which he was taken. I began to place his food on the sidewalk just outside the kitchen door. More cautious than usual, Chopper overcame his fear and made the necessary adjustment.

We were all prepared for the big moment when the maneuver was to take place. Randy was hidden on the front porch, holding a blanket to throw over Chopper while he was eating. Kenny, my husband, was standing behind the kitchen door with a large fish net to put over the bird trapped underneath the blanket.

The first part of this maneuver was successful. Randy, whom the owl recognized as a family member, managed to throw the blanket over Chopper, but before Kenny could secure him with the net, he flew away, lifting the blanket with him. He did not fly very far before leaving the blanket on the ground. At this point, I have to admit that the three of us burst into laughter, tinged with admiration.

We did not see Chopper for three days after that. Then suddenly he was back, sitting on the shelf, looking hopefully toward the house and chop-chopping.

We made no more attempts to force Chopper out of our lives. His confidence restored, he grew more and more tame with the family, but unobtrusive when there were other people in the yard. The only other person he allowed to feed him was our older son, Mark, who was home periodically from college.

By this time we were feeding Chopper dog food instead of hamburger. On Thanksgiving Day we gave him the turkey gizzard, which was not a favorite with anyone in the family. Chopper's enthusiasm was evident, as he begged for more and more. From that time on, I bought chicken gizzards from the grocery store, without telling the butcher what I was going to do with them. He must have thought the family was either wild about chicken gizzards or was having to watch the budget very carefully.

One day, wanting to keep my fingers clean, I gave Chopper his rations on a tablespoon. Chopper leaned over the ledge, nearly losing his balance, and with his gurgling sound, he took the food hungrily, if awkwardly, from the spoon. Except for one time, when he flew away with the spoon, this became the usual method of feeding. Chopper sometimes clacked down on the spoon in his eagerness, missing the food, but this never bothered him much. He simply pulled back, took another sharp, focusing look at the spoon and dived again at its contents. Sometimes he pushed the food to the ground in his haste, and he clucked impatiently while I leaned down, picked up the pieces he had dropped, and offered them to him a second time.

He got so tame that one night when I was taking the garbage to the garbage can, which was located near the detached garage, Chopper, after calling to me, flew at my feet. He landed on my left foot, and because he retracted his talons, he did not even snag my nylon stockings. I stood still until he lost patience and flew back to his perch.

Chopper's relationship to our dog Mac was a matter of some concern. Mac quickly learned that Chopper was a phenomenon to be ignored. I thought the dog was too big to interest the owl as potential food. I had to admit though that Chopper spent a good deal of time perched on the back of a nearby lawn chair, or even on one of the posts that marked a corner of the part of the lawn we had fenced in for Mac's playground. So

I always kept a close eye on events when Mac was outdoors and Chopper was eyeing him.

Randy, on the other hand, believed in taking positive action. One day, when Chopper was staring at Mac, Randy threw a red rubber mouse, a toy of Mac's, which no longer interested him, at Chopper. The mouse brushed against Chopper's wing. The owl looked down at the toy, then picked it up in his talons, and flew into the woods with it. All the rest of that day, we watched as Chopper flew back and forth in the woods with the red rubber mouse tucked firmly in his talons. Although we searched, we never did find the rubber mouse.

On another occasion, when Randy thought the gleam in Chopper's eye, as he watched Mac, was ominous, Randy threw a tennis ball at him. Chopper immediately picked up the ball in his talons and disappeared with it. We did not see Chopper anymore that day, but the following morning, lo and behold, the tennis ball was lying at the foot of one of our oak trees. There was not one speck of fuzz on the ball, which had previously been in good condition.

One of Chopper's activities especially endeared him to me. No matter what time my husband and I returned at night, whether it was nine o'clock on a cold winter's night or two a.m. after a midsummer's party, Chopper always called out a greeting to us. This convinced me that he considered our yard his home territory. We called back to him, and he carried on a conversation with us until we entered the house.

As the weather grew colder, I wondered how Chopper would survive the winter. I did not know of any snug holes in nearby trees where he could seek shelter from the cold north winds. He came for breakfast in the morning with frost on his whiskers and the feathers around his eyes. But he survived.

Chopper grew somewhat more demanding as he grew more tame. My husband and I slept in the front bedroom of the second floor. Beneath the windows to the front was a sloping roof that covered the porch. One morning, as the sun was barely peeking over the horizon I was awakened by a demanding chop-chop sound. How Chopper knew this was where I slept, I do not know, for I had never seen him fly to this position.

But there he was, demanding food. Why should I lie there in bed when I should be feeding him, he appeared to be asking. After all, he had been awake all night, and was now ready to take his breakfast and start catching up on a little sleep.

I was not very happy about this situation. I got up, made shooing motions to the bird, closed the window and let down the blinds. Then I went back to sleep. This happened one more time, and then Chopper got the idea that this waking the mistress up early in the morning was an unproductive activity.

One day the boy who had taken Chopper from his nest called to ask if he could come to see Chopper. I said yes, and soon the boy was at the kitchen window, listening to Chopper call from his favorite perch in a big oak near the back of the yard. When the bird flew to the feeding shelf I went out and fed him. When I returned to the house the boy had a big smile on his face. "This is just the kind of a life I dreamed of for Chopper," he said. He declined my offer for him to try and feed Chopper himself. "It might only confuse him," he said.

Another spectator who was thrilled to see a wild pet such as Chopper was the man who painted our kitchen a few days later.

It was late spring now, and my family reminded me that we would be taking a vacation one of these days. "You've got to stop feeding that darn owl! Let him fend for himself," my husband declared. My thoughts had been running in the same direction. I heard another owl hooting lower down the hill in the woods. Chopper listened intently, but never having learned how to hoot, he did not reply. I observed how closely he focused his eyesight on the squirrels in the yard, and since past experiences had made me very fond of squirrels, I began to fear for their safety. One of these days, instinct would probably take over the job Chopper's parents had been unable to do. I also noticed how the bluejays sometimes harassed him, and how he stoically tried to ignore their actions. This latter activity would, of course, occur whether Chopper learned how to feed himself or not, but I found it distressing to watch.

I began to skip on feeding. Just one a day. Then one every other day. No more gizzards from the butcher shop. Just plain old dog food, the kind he liked least.

Chopper exhibited great flexibility. Okay, if dog food was all he was going to get, he'd settle for that. Seasoned by hunger pangs of sufficient intensity, any food was okay.

As fall approached, I knew he was learning how to hunt, because my wild pet sometimes did not come to me for four or five days. I was happy for him, because he was now leading the kind of life nature had intended for him. However, I did miss that "Welcome home" call that formerly greeted us every night when we had been gone for the evening.

In general, I like to know the truth about things, but I actually wish I had never ever learned the truth about Chopper's fate. He had lived in our yard for ever a year. I am almost certain that I kept Chopper from starving to death, because owls are very dependent upon their parents for several months after they are born. He even let me stroke his feathers once, although we were both apprehensive about this gesture, so I did not repeat it. But I could not teach him how to hoot. His "chop-chop" call remained that of a hungry youngster.

It was the man who had once painted our kitchen for us, and had seen me feed Chopper, who told me what had happened. He was back again, doing some more painting for us.

"I'll bet you miss that big owl," he said to me, as he was drinking a cup of coffee I had prepared for him.

"I surely do," I replied. "I think he must have found a mate and started living the life an owl should live."

"I'm afraid that didn't happen," the painter told me.

"What <u>did</u> happen?" I asked.

"I recognized the owl one day when I was doing some painting for a contractor. The contractor saw the owl too, got his gun and shot him."

"It's hard for me to understand why anyone would do such a thing," I said. "I can understand why some people enjoy hunting. I've always thought it was the joy of being outdoors, enjoying nature, and developing skill at hitting a target that makes hunting a pleasure for some people. But it would not have taken much skill to kill Chopper. Besides, it is against the law to kill an owl."

"I know. But some people are different. This guy told me he knew a man who had his garage framed with the skeletons of owls he had shot."

"I wouldn't care to know such a person."

"Neither would I."

Years later, I find myself missing the sound of Chopper, high in one of our oak trees, calling "Welcome home" to us when we returned at night from going to a movie or visiting with friends. What I cannot comprehend is the "joy" of killing.

Even the killing of a much lower form of life than an owl is hard for me to understand. My older grandson, Christopher, had a salamander for a pet. He had found it on the bank of a small pond located not far from his house. I was taking care of my grandsons at the time. After dinner that night the boys went out to play in the back yard while I did the dishes. It was approaching dusk, time for the boys to come in. I called to them, but there was no answer, nor did I see either of them in the yard where I expected them to be.

I started to call, and when there was no answer, I headed in the direction of the pond. Nolan, the younger of the boys, came running to me, obviously very upset.

"Chris decided to put the salamander where he found it. A big boy came along and tramped on it until it was dead. Chris tried to stop him and couldn't. The salamander was killed. Chris is at the pond, crying." Nolan told me.

Nolan and I hurried toward the pond. Chris was headed in our direction, tears still streaming down his face. "Why did that big boy do that?" he asked me. "I really don't know," I replied. "But some people seem to take pleasure in being mean. I'm so glad you and Nolan aren't that way. How about having a dish of ice cream.

Nolan accepted my offer, but Chris was not hungry after watching the deliberate killing of a creature that for a couple of weeks had been his pet.

COURTSHIP & LOVE

You know spring is here when you see the male cardinal feeding the female who has chosen him as her mate.

Bird courtship can also be a sweet song or a spectacular aerial performance. I well remember the night when six of us stood in an open field at sundown waiting for the exciting slight and son of the woodcock.

"Perhaps he won't come tonight," said the man who had invited us to witness the courtship of the American woodcock.

"He's here! I can hear his whistling wings. He's started his courtship display," his wife said.

Suddenly there he was, flying up and up, in ever widening circles until he reached the peak of his flight to sing his warbling bubbly song of love. Then he descended in a fanciful fluttering flight and called out "Peent, peent."

Was his lady love listening? If so, she made no sound that we could hear. We remained for two more performances by the woodcock and then left, carrying with us the memory of the delightful sounds we had just heard.

At one time, when ours was the only house in a wooded environment that only later became a neighborhood, and after we had first heard the woodcock, we would hear the woodcock's courting sounds each spring in a nearby open field. A friend of ours, Dick Behrens, is an excellent bird photographer. He wanted the sound of a whip-poor-will to accompany a photo he had of one. With excellent sound equipment. Dick managed to record the whip-poor-will's incessant call. Two nights later, he came back and played the recording he had made of this call. Within minutes, his call brought forth a companion, who came close enough to the recorded sound that he all but settled on the equipment. However, with each new house built, the performances became more and more rare, and now there are none.

The same situation exists with the nighthawks. We used to hear their 'beent' as a preliminary to their dive and the following zoom earthward with a whizzing sound of the wings. It is now many years since I have heard or seen a nighthawk. In this case, the reason is probably the use of gas for heating instead of coal.

The whip-poor-will and chuck-will's-widow are still with us however. In Naples, Florida, where my husband and I now spend our winters, I have heard the chuck-will's-widow singing for all he's worth. His call is somewhat weaker than that of his relative.

Twice in my life I have been thrilled by the courtship songs of birds I had never seen. Once was in France, where we were visiting a cousin of mine and her family. I had. requested that my cousin make arrangements for us to stay at a nearby inn. She followed my directions, and after we had visited awhile at their house, she drove us to the inn where she had made reservations for us, in order that we might refresh ourselves for dinner at her house. She must have told the employees there that I was a bird-watcher, for the woman who showed us to our room threw open the windows, which overlooked the Rhone River, and cried out "Nightingale!"

When my cousin returned to pick us up, I told her about this incident, and she replied, "Yes, the nightingales have just arrived." We returned to our room late in the evening. We opened the windows, and sure enough, there was the delightful song of the nightingale. I remember it often with feelings of great pleasure.

On the other occasion, we were in England, not far from Chester. We decided to stay at a bed-and-breakfast establishment, having seen from the highway this very interesting looking stately brick home. There was a room left, the hostess told us, and she prepared some tea and cakes for us. We sat in the living room with her and discussed the possibility that one of my ancestors, according to tradition, was an illegitimate son of a certain famous Englishman. She had an impressive library, and she looked up several references, but could find nothing to substantiate this tradition. We told her we were going to take a walk, and she suggested a country road that went past her house.

As we walked along, I heard a beautiful melody high above us, and looking up, I felt sure that the bird who was singing on the wing was a skylark. The next morning at breakfast, I told our hostess that I had heard a beautiful song from a bird high overhead.

"Oh!" she exclaimed. "You heard our skylark." That ended any doubts I might have had about the identity of the bird singing in the sky.

The most unusual courtship I have ever heard about was told to me and some friends of mine by a farmer who became close friends with a ruffed grouse. A ruffed grouse makes a thumping sound by beating its wings against its breast. It starts out slowly , increasing the tempo until the deep throbbing sounds rather like that of a machine. One fine spring morning this farmer, who lived high on a hill overlooking Lake Pepin, started up his tractor in preparation for plowing his fields. He heard the sound of a ruffed grouse warming up to give his invitation to any females who might be around, and to warn other ruffed grouse that this particular area was his territory.

Because he was interested in birds, the farmer paused to observe the bird's further actions. The grouse came closer and closer. Then he flew away. The next day similar actions took place, and were repeated again the third day. Each time the grouse came closer and closer to the tractor, which possibly struck him as a rather weird looking rival.

Came the day when the grouse hopped into the tractor. The farmer spoke gently to him and in time the grouse trusted the man sufficiently so that he sat on the man's lap. This action continued until snows came and the grouse was heard no more.

The next spring, the farmer was delighted to find himself remembered by the grouse, and the man and the bird continued their friendship.

Then came the day when the grouse did not respond to the sound of the tractor. Day after day the man started his machine up, but no bird came. At last he had to face the truth. Some larger creature, most likely a fox, had made himself a meal of the farmer's pet.

The courtship of merganser ducks is spectacular. Last year, from the chickee house at the end of the boardwalk of Bay Forest in Naples, my husband and I watched in amazement at the sight of a large area of the bay the chickee house overlooks, where the water was foaming into small fountains. About two dozen mergansers were leaping into the air, splashing wildly before returning to the surface of the water.

Some birds, such as swans and geese, mate for life others may choose a second mate for the season, or even for each brood. Wrens are not monogamous, but the power of love binds them closely together when they are courting or raising a family. One day I heard a thud against the side of the house. My reaction to such a sound is dismay, for usually it means that a bird has bumped against the house and injured, or even killed, itself. I walked from the porch, where I have been reading, and looked around, but noticed nothing unusual. Forty-five minutes later I was about to enter the house when I saw a small brown object on the deck outside of the kitchen. A bird? Yes. My heart sank as I recognized one of the little wrens that was nesting in one of our birdhouses.

It was on its side, apparently lifeless. But a closer look revealed that she was still breathing. Her breathing was spasmodic, her whole body heaving with each breath. Her eyes were closed and a loose, whitish feather protruded from the right one. Was she injured so badly that she would not recover? With aching heart. I wondered what I could do to help. I decided that at this point I could be most helpful by noninterference.

A few minutes later there is a burst of wren song. Looking at the deck I discover that the injured bird is now erect and has turned herself about to face the direction from which the song is coming. The trills of her mate, sitting on a nearby branch, continue to fill the air. A short time later the accident victim opens her eyes. And not long after that she flies to sit beside her mate. Safe! After resting briefly, they fly together to the box which contains their nest.

The power of love had proved itself, as it so often does. Who knows whether the injured wren would have recovered if she had not been stimulated to do so by desire to join her mate. Certainly he was doing all he could to call her back to life with the vigor of his song.

A number of days later, I was on the trail that leads from our house through a wooded area and a small gully which separates our house from what was at that time our garden. Once I reached the wooded area, I heard a conversation between four members of a wren family. I have no doubt that this is the family which occupied our wren house, and whose mother had survived injury. The four wrens were within a few feet of one another, and not much higher than my head. They were not singing and they were not scolding. The only term that described their vocalizing was "chatter".

One wren would chatter awhile, and was answered by another. At times their conversation became so exciting that all four were chattering at once. I was sufficiently intrigued so that I stood there awhile listening. When I left the wooded area and reached the garden, the conversation ceased, so I could only suppose that the subject was me.

Most birds make a number of different sounds. Bluejays, for instance, especially young ones begging for food, come up with some sounds so weird you have to see the swelling of the bird's throat at the same time the sound is made to be sure it is really a bluejay.

I observed another case of a bird's love of its mate when I saw a female grackle who had been killed on a road near our house. A crow was attempting to make a meal of her, but the grackle's mate was fiercely defending her body by repeatedly driving the crow away.

My husband and I have great opportunity for watching ducks at Bay Point Park in Red Wing, where we usually take our daily walk. The park is beside the Mississippi River near the place where the river has the sharpest curve in its whole length. Many of the ducks remain here the year round, since warm water from the cooling towers of the Prairie Island Nuclear plant keep the river open at all times.

It was the middle of November when I was watching six mallards by the boathouses that adjoin the park on the bay side. They were swimming two by two. One male was continually dipping his head in the direction of another mallard in what could only be a courtship gesture. My husband used to be a duck hunter, and I called his attention to this matter. Yes, he said, it was definitely a courtship gesture. Nearby was another pair of mallards. The green-headed male was dipping his head playfully in the water. This time the object of his affections was a female.

As we turned the curve and began to parallel the river at a closer angle, we spotted another pair. One male was ducking his head in courtship to another male.

Were they practicing for next spring, just as some young wrens practice nest building at the end of the season?

Parental Care

Of all the birds I love, bluebirds take first place. When the field next to our house was a cornfield, with the sound of dry corn rustling in the late summer breeze, and the ecstatic melody of the meadowlark singing, I spent much time observing the bluebird family which annually built a nest in the bluebird house we nailed for them near the top of a post.

Year after year the bluebird family accepted us as an innocent part of the environment. So imagine my surprise when I returned from downtown one day, parked the car in front of the garage and emerged to find myself under assault by my formerly friendly bluebirds. They swooped at me, barely missing my hair. What had happened? I guessed the answer when I realized that there were not just two bluebirds, the male and the female, but five of them. It was the parents who were assaulting me, and their reason for doing so was to protect their newly fledged young ones from any possible harm. I took the hint and hurriedly entered the house. I did not see these bluebirds until the following spring.

Meanwhile, I kept remembering how delighted my husband and I were, soon after we built our house in its large, wooded lot, to discover that the bluebirds were making use of the house we had put in place for them on the fence post. To begin with, we faced the house west, so that we could better observe the comings and goings of the birds. After four days, with no luck, we were told by friends that the house should face east, because that is the direction bluebirds prefer. We turned the house about, and within a couple of hours, we had the tenants we wanted.

One day, tired from working in our new house, my husband and I gave up thoughts of going out in the boat, and instead, put up a couple of chaise lounges in the shade almost underneath the bluebird house. A blind person could easily tell when one of the parent bluebirds returned with food. The young ones inside set up a chattering sound you could not miss, once you learned to identify it.

Although the bluebirds were undisturbed when I sat in this spot one day the previous week, the mother was now upset over the fact that there were two spectators. She sat on the barbed wire fence close to the post on which the bluebird house was located. With an insect crammed in her mouth, she scolded us.

She was obviously afraid to enter her home while we were watching. Edging close to it, she would then panic and fly up to perch on the power line above the wooden box containing her young ones.

In a couple of minutes the father came with food, entered the birdhouse and came out after a minute or so. Still the mother hesitated. The father flew to sit close to her on the power line . In dulcet tones they conversed softly about the matter for awhile. Then the father flew to the field beyond for more provisions.

The mother flies to the fence again. Closer. Pause. Closer. Now at last she goes into the nest. She does not stay there for a minute or so, as the father did. She pops in and out so fast I have to wonder if she tossed the food, hoping it would hit an open mouth.

I count the number of trips each bird makes in the next hour. The male makes fourteen trips to the female's four. Ordinarily they make about the same number of trips with food for the young.

While we watch, a pine siskin flies down and perches right next to the birdhouse. He pokes his nose into the house. The father bluebird dives from the power line in a fighting mood, and the pine siskin retreats to a spot on the fence farther from the birdhouse. The bluebird, pursuing, sits right beside him. The pine siskin takes the hint and leaves the area. Male bluebirds are very aggressive about driving rivals and predators away from their nest. They fight with sparrows who want the house. I once watched a bluebird chase a red squirrel out of the yard three times before the squirrel decided to do his hunting elsewhere.

Repeatedly, I have seen the male and female bluebird sitting on the wire above their birdhouse and talk gently to one another. When the power line was set up on our lot line, I objected to its presence. There wasn't anything I could do about it, because we definitely wanted the utilities. I found myself wishing those lines could have been buried. I felt the same way about the barbed wire fence. But this one was here, and we did need some kind of a fence to mark the separation of our land and the field beyond it.

As it turned out, the power line and the fence were great assets for one who was very fond of bird watching, as I was. The bluebirds in particular loved to perch on both the power line and the barbed wire fence before going into their house. Other birds used the wire as well. When they sit there and sing, they are in very plain sight, easy to identify. This also makes learning their songs much easier.

Interesting is the fact that an observer once saw the young of the first brood help the widowed male bluebird feed the young of the second brood.

The year after I had first seen the successful raising of a bluebird family, I had a lot of opportunity to watch bird parenting, and I observed that cardinals and bluejays have quite different styles in caring for their young. There had been young bluejays in the backyard for about a week now. They look just like the adults, but the fluttering of the wings and the loud, pleading cries for food distinguish them.

One day I watched as a father bluejay began to wean its young one. The fledgling was sitting in a jack pine near the feeder, whimpering for food. Its parent flew to the feeder, picked up a sunflower seed in its beak, flew to the young one, and held out the seed in his beak. Just as the eager young one reached for it, the parent flew to the ground beneath the feeder.

Its offspring followed, still pleading. But the parent ignored its cries and swallowed the seed himself. Soon the young one was tilting its head this way and that for a better look at the seeds on the ground. Then he flew to the base of the feeder, where there were always a number of seeds lying. He picked one up in his beak. While he was so occupied the parent flew away, leaving the youngster in the process of supplying his own needs.

At least a week before the young bluejays appeared, a male cardinal was in the yard feeding a brown-headed cowbird. I remembered hearing the melodic call of a cowbird and looking out the window to see a male and a female cowbird at the base of the feeder earlier in the season. I also remember hoping at that time that the female had not placed its eggs in the nests of any of my favorite birds, such as the cardinal and the rose- breasted grosbeak.

A more devoted parent than this male cardinal feeding the baby cowbird I had never seen. The juvenile cowbird sat in the jack pine, with feeble but incessant cries, while the cardinal made trip after trip to the feeder and returned to place the seed in the mouth of his foster child. In all probability the cowbird, which develops more rapidly than the host young, had pushed the young cardinals out of the nest or starved them by hogging all the food.

Two days later the male cardinal was still feeding the young cowbird, even at times when the cowbird was sitting at his side on the platform of the feeder. The unfortunate parent, unaware that he has been duped into feeding the young of another species, made no attempt to force the young bird to become independent.

Only occasionally do I see a female cardinal at the feeder during this phase of family life. On one of these occasions the male chased her away. Not content with chasing her from the feeder, he drove her out of the yard. I could only suppose that this particular female was not his mate.

For awhile there were two male cardinals caring for young cowbirds at our main feeder. I puzzled for quite some time over the significance

and not the female, feeding the young foster offspring? Could it be that the female recognizes that the young is not a cardinal? In other years I have watched young cardinals being fed by their mothers.

I would have enjoyed being able definitely to report the superiority of female over male cardinals, in this respect, but I decided to check the Audubon Society Encyclopedia of North American Birds. Here I read that the male cardinal cares for the first brood while the female is incubating eggs of the second brood. So the matter was explained not by sexual superiority but by sexual cooperation.

I often see large groups of cowbirds congregated at a park that adjoins the Mississippi River. I wonder if this small flock contains parents and their young. If so, how do they recognize one another? Fortunately, some birds do recognize cowbird eggs and destroy them by building a new layer of nest over the alien eggs. Otherwise we might be overrun by cowbirds, since the female brown-headed cowbird may lay ten to twelve eggs during the nesting season.

There is a heron rookery which can be reached only by boat, and which is not too far from where we live. It is late June, and though there is not as much activity here as there was two weeks ago, it is still a busy place. The cries of young ones from a couple of hundred nests creates a continual pulsing sound, low and hoarse. The odor is not for the squeamish, and it is well to have the head covered. The nests show up plainly because high water has killed most of the big trees in this area. Some of the young are now standing upright in the nests, looking like branches in the dead trees. Among the heron nests are a small number of common egret nests. We watch as an egret parent lands near a nest right above us. Three fluffy white young ones, already large enough to be showing above the rim of the large nest, jockey for position. The adult hops to the edge of the nest and opens its beak. The nearest baby egret sticks its beak inside the adults beak, and with spasmodic motions of the neck, the adult regurgitates the food for the young to eat. This action is repeated several times. As far as we can see, only one infant is fed on this trip. The adult flies away. Shortly afterwards the young ones, still restless, start practicing this beak-to-beak feeding on one another.

There is one tragic event that we witness but can do nothing about. Underneath the nest area is a baby great blue heron. Apparently it has fallen out of the nest, probably in an excess of eagerness to get its share of the food. You might expect that one of the parents, hearing the poor young one's cries for help, would feed it as it stood in water that came halfway up his legs. But, since he was out of the nest, he was completely ignored by his parents, and we knew that the end result would be starvation of this unfortunate young one.

My husband and I have much opportunity to watch duck families as we take our daily walk in Bay Point Park, which stretches along the Mississippi River. Almost every year one or more duck families are raised in the small boat harbor, which adjoins the park. Some of these families are raised in the interior of the boathouses. A friend of ours was startled one day when he opened the door to his boathouse and found a mallard hen and drake taking their leave of a coil of rope on the boathouse floor. A few days later the mother brooded her clutch on that same coil of rope. The owner was careful not to disturb her.

Came the day when he discovered her in the water near the boathouse with three young ones trailing close behind her. She deserted the other eleven eggs in the nest, since the three in the water definitely needed her attention. Our friend, Cal Eastlund, held the eggs up to his ear and found that some sounded as if liquid was sloshing about in them, while others gave forth with a soft "peep, peep ". He broke open one of the eggs that sounded liquid and found that it showed no sign of any development.

The eggs which seemed to contain chicks he entrusted to the care of two women who have a hobby of rescuing birds and animals in need of help. They put the eggs in an incubator and successfully cared for them until they were adults.

On another occasion, we were in our boat, turning at the end of the boom, headed for our boathouse.

"Watch out for the baby duckling," a woman called to us.

Ahead of us was a mallard hen with one very small, very fluffy duckling swimming close behind her. As we watched, the mother climbed up on the porch of a boathouse across from ours. She quacked loudly for the duckling to follow her. The duckling gave a thin little call of distress. The porch is at least eighteen inches from the surface of the water, and there is no possibility of his being able to jump up that distance. The mother continued quacking, then leaned down and tried to pull him up with her beak, but was unable to do this. The cries of the duckling were pathetic. He swam back and forth below his mother, unable to join her. She paced back and forth on the porch with excited quacks, perplexed as to what she should do. At last she jumped into the water beside him and they swam off together. We wondered where they would spend the night.

After observing this incident, I think I know why the mallard mother in the Eastlund boat house gave up brooding eleven of her eggs. Three ducklings must have hatched in one day. She coaxed them into the water, and when evening came she found they could not get back into the boathouse. So she stayed with the young ones who had hatched and had to abandon those that were still in the egg. She was forced to choose between brooding the remainder of the eggs or caring for the chicks already hatched.

One day, when we were at Round Lake in Wisconsin, a group of us watched as one lone duckling tried to join the seven other young ones in the group. The mother hen drove him off with angry squawks and jabs of the beak. The alien duckling waited awhile and then tried again. The mother duck repeated her "get out of here" antics, and once again the orphan swam away. This happened seven times and finally the orphan gave up and wandered away.

One year we noticed a rather sloppy nest in a young tree in our back yard. Observation convinced us that it was a green heron nest. We were surprised to find the nest in that location because we are about a mile away from any water. Yet the young ones were definitely living on fish, because we found the skeletons of fish underneath the nest and along the trail that led from our house to the nest.

One night a bad storm blew up, and in the morning we found most of the twigs that had formed the nest lying on the ground beneath where the nest had been. There were three young ones. Two of them were dead, but the third young one was still living. I picked him up, put him in a cardboard box and put a bit of fish in the box for him to eat. A few hours later, I discovered that he had managed to fly out of the box and was sitting higher up in the tree than the nest had been. I kept an eye out for him the next few days. He was able to fly the next day, and was in the general area for three more days. So I had the satisfaction of knowing that one of the young ones had survived the storm.

For some time I puzzled over the fact that some wrens build nests so late in the season that there was really no possibility that a family could be raised in time to join the necessary migration to the South. Then I learned that the ones building the nests this late in the season were the young ones. Apparently they are practicing up for next year.

There are a number of loons on Gull Lake, Minnesota, and our family is one of those who think the calls of the loon are delightful to hear. One day my younger granddaughter, Kara, was watching a loon that was swimming near the front of the house. It looked to her as if there was some kind of a growth, like a tumor, on the back of the bird. With the help of binoculars, she 1earned that the "growth" on the back of the loon was the baby loon. The youngster was getting a free ride.

In general, people in my hometown, Red Wing, Minnesota, have warm feelings in their hearts for birds and animals, especially birds. Maybe this is because the scenery around the town is lovely, and people who enjoy beauty are inclined to love birds. A prime example of such an attitude was exhibited by the Vogel family, which had a houseboat, a treasure in which the parents had taken their honeymoon. When the family discovered a mallard hen had established a nest in the "Nelly Bly" a sign was put up on the boat, "Under quarantine", and the boat was not used until the mother hen and her ducklings left the houseboat for a more natural environment.

Family ties of ducks are strong. Even when the ducklings are as large as the mother, they may still be with her. It is common too see a number of half-grown ducklings swimming together in a line, with no adult in attendance. When danger threatens, the mother calls her duckling to her with loud, insistent quacks, and they are quick to obey.

I have a granddaughter who, at the age of ten, already had an earned reputation as an expert on birds. She explains her knowledge of birds by saying "I'm PASSIONATE about birds." She was patiently watching a family of geese making their way from a pond at the bottom of a slope behind her house. As they climbed the hill toward the house, the gander led the procession, goslings behind him, Mother Goose bringing up the rear.

Sudden danger! A snake is wiggling its way toward the geese. The goslings would make a tempting meal for this snake. Regan watched the mother spread her wings, hissing at the snake and calling the goslings to cluster under her for protection. They did so. The gander stretched his neck as far as it would go, hissed fiercely, opened his beak, thrust forward with all his might, and cut the garter snake in two. Being a parent sometimes requires great courage, in the world of birds as well as humans.

SURVIVAL

We are on the way back to the house after planting some pine tree seedlings. I follow my husband down the narrow, wooded trail. My eyes are on the ground and at first I do not believe what I see. A woodcock! I've seen so many pictures of this bird that I have no trouble recognizing it, even though this is the first one I have encountered. It is sitting about two feet off the path and it is so motionless I think perhaps this is a stuffed bird someone has put here for a joke. Then I observe a slight motion of the black, shiny eyeball.

I call softly to my husband to turn around and see the woodcock. Skeptically he looks where I am pointing. The bird is sitting among brown oak leaves, and its stocky body, feathered with various shades of brown, is so beautifully camouflaged my husband cannot see it. I lean forward slightly and point. Now at last, though the bird does not move, it is visible to him. We back off, go into the house, and call a friend who is an excellent nature photographer. By the time we return, the bird has left.

Birds are not alone in remaining motionless, hoping the human intruder or prey-seeker will go away without seeing them. I almost stepped on a nest once that contained a baby cottontail rabbit. He was about five inches long and remained motionless while my husband and I observed him. His ears were so erect and tense that they almost touched one another. Not until I got about a foot and a half away did he take off, white tail flashing as he took shelter close to the trunk of a pine.

Hunters say you almost have to step on a woodcock to flush it. "Freezing" is a method employed by various birds and animals who depend heavily on camouflage for survival. The bittern holding its head straight up so it will look like just another weed, and the fawn lying motionless on the forest floor while enemies pass by unsuspecting are both using the same technique as the woodcock.

Sometimes freezing is so inappropriate, it is almost ridiculous, as in the case of the whip-poor-will who perched on the hood of our car in the garage, as if it were a hood ornament. In the darkness of the garage, we did not notice him until the car was in motion. After all, who thinks to check for a whip-poor-will on the car hood? My husband stopped the car just outside the garage and I got out to inspect the bird. He remained utterly motionless. Even his eyes were closed. Whip-poor-wills are, of course, nocturnal birds, but obviously a healthy, sleeping bird would be wakened by the motion of the car. I learned later that birds which depend on camouflage sometimes narrow their eyes to a slit in a desperate effort to escape detection.

We thought this bird must be dying, for why else would he make no effort to escape? We didn't realize he thought he was well hidden, and he didn't realize how glaringly obvious he was on the car hood in the morning sunlight. (A whip-poor-will who managed to lose himself in a china store took his place among some porcelain figures and his presence remained unnoticed until at last he moved.)

Since my husband and I had appointments to keep, we decided to put the bird in a clothes basket and leave it in the garage until our return. He should then be safe from predators and perhaps we could nurse him back to health when we returned.

Confinement in the clothes basket galvanized the whip-poor-will into action. There was a flurry of wings. I tipped the basket sideways so that he could more easily escape. Whoosh! Up and away! He landed spread-eagled on the branch of a spruce, about ten feet off the ground. To the right of him, separated by several inches, were two of his gorgeous white-tipped tail feathers.

We expected to find him dead when we returned. However, an observer who was working in our house at the time said that about ten minutes after we left the bird flew away, missing tail feathers notwithstanding.

One day, on a walk along the beach of the Gulf of Mexico, I observed a group of pelicans fishing. As I watched I noticed several smaller birds, gulls and terns, keeping close company with the pelicans. One gull even rode on top of a pelican. It did not take long for me to notice that once in a while a pelican would lose his fish meal while turning it around so that he could swallow it head first. (Otherwise the fish fins would scratch its throat.) Even when the pelican did not lose the fish, small bits of it might escape the big bird's mouth. It was then that the gull would get the scraps of food it wanted without having to make much effort in obtaining his meal. Since then, I have often noticed gulls, and sometimes terns, teaming up with a pelican for an easy meal.

Most birds vary their meals by the availability of certain kinds of food. Bluebirds eat a side variety of insects, including cutworms and grasshoppers. Later in the season, they will take advantage of the numerous berries that have ripened. Orioles will feed hungrily at the hummingbird feeder until it is time to feed their young, which apparently need protein. The Orioles will return to the hummingbird feeder for a brief period before leaving for the South. I have seen osprey feeding on fish that were about the same size as the bird. They are often seen working on their meal high in a branch of a dead tree.

A gull with wind-ruffled feathers is at a disadvantage if it has to fly rapidly in order to escape danger. That is why when you see a group of gulls sitting on the beach, they will all be facing the wind.

One day I saw a willet who couldn't keep up with the other birds of its kind. It would run along with them for a short distance, then stop and hold its left leg up in the air. It would hop a few steps, and then fly to catch up with the others. This performance was repeated several times while I watched. Three days later, I saw two willets sitting down close to the water's edge. As I approached, the birds began to run. One of them was forced to limp after a few steps.

The other one waited until the injured one caught up. Then the two of them flew away together. What caused the uninjured bird to tie up with the bird who had to limp? It was early March, so perhaps it was an example of mating activity. Or was it simply compassion, as is sometimes observed in animals such as porpoises.

The bird with the limp reminded me of a pheasant who was incapacitated in a similar fashion. I was sitting on the porch one day when my attention was captured by the slight crackling noise of dead grasses being pushed aside. I looked up from my reading, and saw a couple of young pheasants in the yard. As I watched, a third one entered from the adjoining field, where wheat was recently thrashed, and then a fourth one. They were coming under the barbed wire fence, over tall, native grass that had been flattened at that spot. I continued to watch until eleven had come single file into sight. They were feeding along the fence line in a part of the yard we had left wild. As they advanced, my vision of them was partially obscured by the pine trees and tall grasses in between, but I could see that they stretched their wings occasionally and sometimes flew for a short distance. I went over by the fence for a better view. Most of them were under the pine trees now, feeding on the ground. Whenever they came to an open space they ran rapidly until they were again under cover.

The birds were now about ten weeks old. They were purchased from a game farm by Scott Klabunde, a boy who lived across the road from us. He built a shelter for the original twenty-five, and gave them tender care until their size resulted in overcrowding. When he discovered one morning that two of the birds had been pecked to death by the others, he knew he must let them go. As he opened the door and let them out, he thought perhaps he had seen the last of them. But the next morning they were all back, enjoying the food and water he had left outdoors by the shelter. Several of the birds were sitting on the roof of the shelter.

Soon they were scrounging for themselves, having discovered that the grapes that grew on the grapevines that climbed the barbed wire that separated our yard from the farm beyond were delicious. Scott and I watched twelve of them one hot noon until they had their fill of the fruit. They then settled down for a nap under the shade and tent-like shelter of the grapevine.

A week later the group was still keeping together by a series of small peeping sounds. One cock called much louder than the others, and when he called the others came. Scott told me that there were two such leaders in the original twenty-five. The cocks are now beginning to develop the gorgeous colors that will distinguish them as adults. There is a red ring around the eyes, patches of iridescent green showing on the head, and soft rust color on the breast. Both males and females have short tails at this stage of development.

The remaining birds of the twenty-three released are roaming the area in groups. We hear reports of cars stopping to let four or six juvenile pheasants cross the road. It is likely that some of the youngsters have already met violent deaths. The flock I see now in my yard has one crippled member. Her leg had been broken and had healed crooked. Soon she was not with this group anymore. I am almost certain that she did not reach maturity. The odds for a crippled bird are surely small.

It pays to investigate when bluejays call their alarm. I leave my typewriter to investigate an alarm sounded by several jays and discover a Cooper's hawk sitting on a bare spot on a jack pine limb in our front yard. She is tearing chunks of meat from the body of a junco she is holding in her talons against the tree limb. I have an excellent view of the event, since she is only about twenty feet away from the window where I am watching her. The hawk is large for its species, so I decide it must be a female.

My sympathy is almost always with the underdog, in this case, the junco, but I must admit that this hawk is a very beautiful bird. The sleek, bluish gray of the back and head, the warm horizontal bars of the breast, and the rich lower covert feathers at the base of the narrow, banded tail make it an extremely colorful bird. And she has to eat or die of starvation. She is alert, but not timid. After each bite she raises her head and looks about her. At one point I tap repeatedly on the window, hoping she will fly so I can get a better look at her tail. The tapping receives her attention but she decides to ignore it.

The poor junco is going down the hawk's gullet in chunks. Every now and then a feather falls to the ground. I watch as the hawk pulls loose chunks of intestine and see how she struggles to swallow parts of the skeleton. The process take quite awhile. I have been watching now for about half an hour.

Most of the bluejays left after their original scolding, but one bold fellow returns to torment the hawk. The jay flies from one spot to another, circling the hawk, and landing in positions about two or three feet distant. The hawk keeps a sharp eye on the jay.

I can hardly believe it! The jay flies just above the hawk, swoops down and actually strikes the hawk's back. The hawk stops eating, raises its wings a trifle, and prepares for flight. The jay settles one foot away, still scolding. Then he flies in back of the hawk and lands in another spot a foot away. Not until he tires of this activity does the jay fly away and the hawk begin eating again.

There is very little left of the junco now. I decide to try for a picture. I get out the camera, focus it on the hawk, who is staring fiercely at me with its golden iris surrounding the black pupil. Slowly I begin to open the window. This is a mistake. The hawk flies away.

The hawks do not always catch their prey. One day I watched a hawk trying unsuccessfully to capture a grackle. The grackle veers and dips and climbs, but the hawk is within inches of capturing its prey. The two birds, flying very low, reach the wooded ravine and pass from my range of vision. However, a couple of minutes later the hawk, a beautiful bird with its long, narrow tail and short, rounded wings, flies toward the road. He is flying high now and this time he is surrounded by eight grackles who take turns diving at him. He is sufficiently annoyed to swerve at them occasionally, but he misses each time. He settles high in a large tree that stands by itself on some wasteland beyond the cornfield. He is still hungry, and for him the struggle for this day's survival is not over. The grackles, having chased him away from their nesting area, call off the pursuit.

A sad event happened in our area on a day in the fall hunting season. A number of tundra swans passed over the Mississippi bottomland about dawn on a cold November morning. The hunters thought they were honking like geese and shot. When the birds fell and the hunters discovered their mistake, they took two of the swans that were still alive to the veterinarian. This was an act of courage, since there is a very large fine for shooting swans.

One of the birds suffered only a broken wing; the other was more seriously injured and was not expected to survive.

However, in December, we discovered that the two swans were swimming together in the waters of Colvill Park, where they were recuperating. They were keeping company with the semi-tame ducks that live year-round in this bay that is warmed by water from the cooling towers of a nearby power plant.

A short time later, after some severely cold weather, the swans left. Shivering with cold, I applaud their good judgment. One of the swans could now fly perfectly well. The other could fly, but awkwardly.

Birds fly together for safety as well as for companionship. One evening in September, my husband and I were out in the yard working when we heard a loud racket overhead. A big flock of birds was flying over us. We were puzzled at first by their identity. They were large birds that were flying with their heads drawn back. At last we were able to see a large, orange, telltale beak. White pelicans! They are not seen very frequently in our area. One of the birds, doubtless a young one, was far behind the others. He was squawking for all he was worth. We wished him well, and wondered what would happen to him if he did not catch up with the group.

I once found a hummingbird in our yard that was too weak to fly. It had stayed in Minnesota long after all the other hummingbirds had left for a warmer climate. I cradled him in my hand, put him on our front porch, which was several steps up from the ground, and placed a dish of sugar water with him. The next morning he was gone, and there were no loose feathers or any other signs of struggle, so I hope he made it the rest of the way.

In a secluded bay known only to boaters and wildlife a flock of turkey vultures soars clockwise a couple of hundred feet above the beach. There are thirteen of them soaring in a circle that veers gradually toward the center of the lake. A lone vulture approaches the circle from the west and effortlessly finds a position on the formation. Two more join the group in similar fashion. I watch for perhaps fifteen minutes, and although the birds occasionally tilt to right or left, not a single one gives so much as one flap of the wings. There is very little wind, and it is a hot July day. The rising of warm air must create enough of an updraft to keep the vultures sustained in an effortless glide, their wings curved slightly upward from the horizontal for as long as they wish to soar. It is obvious that they are waiting for some unfortunate creature to die.

Even turkey vultures will not eat a carcass that has decayed to a really foul -smelling stage, as we learned from friends of ours. A number of years ago Dick Behrens, an expert nature photographer, decided he wanted some film on turkey vultures feeding. He notified the local veterinarian that he would like to use a dead animal as bait. The cooperative veterinarian soon called to say that he had a dead calf which could be used for this purpose.

This was mid-week, and Dick was not able to spend a day in a blind until Sunday, so he decided to bury the calf in the sand of a bay that can only be reached by boat. He enlisted the help of his wife, my husband and yours truly for this project. He had to work until 9 p.m. Setting out in the cool of the evening we loaded the calf, wrapped in a white cotton blanket covered with plastic, into the boat. We felt fortunate that no one was at the yacht club to ask what the heck we were doing.

We journeyed down river until we reached the isolated bay where the calf was to be taken. The water in the bay was low, so in order to reach the desired spot, we had to wade in the muck, pulling the boat. On the sandy beach, the men dug a hole without much difficulty. At this point we were glad of the darkness and the loneliness of the spot, for it would have been difficult to explain to anyone other than a serious birder or dedicated nature photographer the object of our expedition. With effort, we got the calf out of the boat and its protective covering and placed the calf in the hole, and then the men promptly covered the hole with sand. That done, we took the boat into Lake Pepin and had a drink.

Alas, all was in vain. Came Sunday, with a beautiful July sun, perfect for photographing vultures. My husband and I had the good fortune

to be away for the weekend. Dick and Dorothy uncovered the carcass, which was now swollen to grotesque proportions.

The stench was unbearable. Not a vulture came near that carcass, not that day or any day thereafter. Nor did the other carrion eaters come near. The calf remained a blotch on the landscape until finally time and nature, with help from insects, reduced it to bare bones. It was a long while before Dick and Dorothy were able to enjoy meat.

For years I was a member of a bicycle group. The number of women varied from three to eighteen. What all members of the "core group" had in common was a love of nature. Meeting Monday mornings at a spot where we could park our cars, we each carried a bag lunch, decided on a destination (not too far if it threatened rain, a longer distance if the weather was cooperative) and started out. The time we spent was primarily determined by how many wild flowers and birds we stopped to identify, and how long was spent enjoying the picnic spot we had chosen for our lunch.

One day, on a road that followed a small Wisconsin river, we stopped to watch the last stages of the birth of a colt. The afterbirth was lying on the ground, and the pony was unsteadily struggling to its feet. The horse was licking its young one, establishing the bonding process. We stood and watched for some quite some time, enjoying the sight of a new life, and the establishment of the mother-offspring bond.

Farther down the road we stopped again. We had witnessed life. This time we witnessed life and death. The frogs were enjoying a very noisy mating season. The whole pond was quivering with the motion of males mounting females, and sometimes mistakenly mounting other males.

The sound of their mating calls blended into a symphony of sound. Enjoying the whole process tremendously was a great blue heron who stood to one side of the pond and gobbled down the frogs as fast as he could swallow them. The frogs seemed totally unaware of his presence, and the heron was having the feast of his life.

On another occasion, a field mouse thought he was in seventh heaven. He was in the clean garbage can in which we store sunflower seeds. When I was preparing to refill the sunflower feeder, I noticed that the cover of the pail was slightly open. A raccoon, I thought. Raccoons are very clever at opening cans containing seeds. Eventually, we learned how to tie the cover on by means of a chain secured by a clasp, and far enough away from the house wall so that they cannot brace themselves against the house.

By the time I arrived home and discovered the mouse in the bottom of the near-empty can, the mouse was frantic. How should I get him out?

The safest way, I decided, was to tip the can until he was able to run for freedom. I began to tip the can, but, panic-stricken, he started to climb in the wrong direction. I lowered it further. With a courage born of desperation, he ran toward me and out of the can, whence he beat it toward the woods for all he was worth. I never told this story to anyone because I knew the general reaction from other people would be decidedly negative.

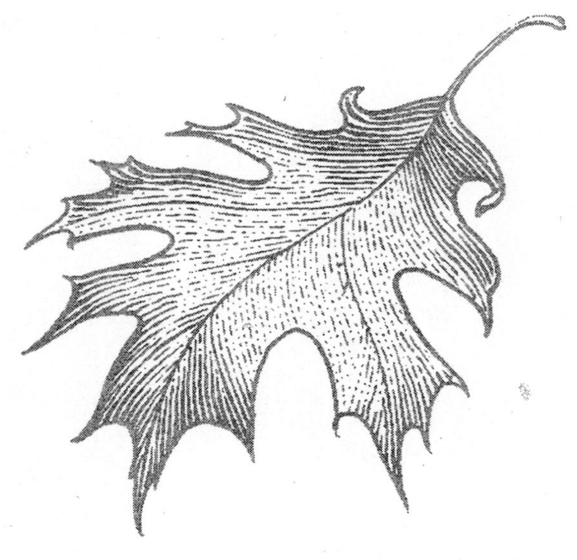

BEHAVIOR PATTERNS

I wonder if birds do not have an instinct for falling barometric pressure which was, as humans, have lost. My parents were in a cabin at a resort on Cass Lake, where huge Norway pines are spectacular in their height and beauty. A fierce storm struck this area in the 1940s. It moved the cabin in which my parents were staying off its foundation. For several days after the storm, the occupants of the resort, Norway Pine Beach, were stranded. A number of the enormous pines had fallen over the narrow road leading to the highway. My mother often remarked about the fact that the martins were flying about rapidly and erratically the evening before the storm hit. It seems possible that the birds were aware of the change in air pressure and that they were disturbed by a foreboding that danger was approaching.

You may have noticed that if pieces of bread, or other food, are tossed to a gull, it will soon be joined by a large group of others of its kind. How do the birds know about this food? For one thing, the way the first gull flies to the food is a signal. Then too, the gulls give a loud, high-pitched cry that carries far and this attracts other gulls.

Gulls seem very sociable in many ways. If there are several gulls in the area, they will usually be found facing the same direction. This is because they need to face the wind when they decide to fly. But in other ways, the gulls are not so sociable. There have been cases where one gull will eat the eggs of another gull, who is temporarily absent, and the baby gull that ends up with the wrong brood may not live to remember the event.

Flight patterns are often the key to identifying birds. I once asked my husband, who used to be a duck hunter, how he could tell that a duck flying overhead was a mallard and not a wood duck. He replied that mallards beat their wings very fast, whereas a wood duck flies more slowly and closer to the ground, with its head moving up and down.

An owl flies so silently that one might fly by you on a dark night and you would not even know it. The owl needs this kind of flight because it hunts primarily at night, and it needs to approach its prey without waking its potential meal.

Of the small birds that fly above you in the daytime, the goldfinch has a deep undulating flight that makes identification easy.

One sunny day in May I was waiting for some friends to arrive. The view from the spot where I waited was gorgeous, and the day was warm and cloudless. The land where I sat sloped downward to the wide spot in the Mississippi which is called Lake Pepin. My attention was drawn skyward by the flight of what I believed must be a hawk. Because I saw it only in silhouette against the sky, I did not know what kind of hawk it was. But his or her flight caught my attention because it would glide for half a minute or so, without tilting, even though there was a rather brisk wind. Suddenly it would stop and remain in one position by fluttering its wings much as a tern would do when it spots a fish.

The hawk must have sighted some potential food, such as a mouse, but each time, after fluttering for several seconds, it would glide a long distance again, then stop to flutter. For awhile it was joined by another bird of the same species, which flew around it in a dance, up and over and around. The bird that was looking for food paid no attention to its suitor, and after awhile the second bird gave up after it became convinced that he was getting no response. I later learned from a bird expert that the bird flight I described to him was not that of a hawk but of an American kestrel.

In a Minnesota autumn cedar waxwings sometimes begin to fly very erratically. The birds are drunk from eating crab apples in which the sugar has turned to alcohol.

Sociability towards others of its kind, or towards humans varies a great deal. Chickadees are so accustomed to being fed by humans that they can, with patience, be trained to come and take food from one's hand. Gulls will also flock to anyone who is tossing pieces of bread for them to devour.

Ovenbirds, on the other hand, are so secretive that they nested in the woods beside our house year after year, and I did not realize it until I found a dead one that had bumped into a window. This has happened two more times, in spite of my efforts to make the windows visible to them. This always happens about the time the young ones are learning to fly. I have now learned that when I hear a bird singing "Teacher, teacher" it is the ovenbird that is calling.

Identifying birds by their song is easiest when you can see the bird's throat swelling as the sound comes out. But this is an opportunity that doesn't comes too often. I have listened to tapes of bird songs and have found some of them very helpful. I have learned that the song of a chipping sparrow, if you can call it a song, is an insect-like sound, only louder. He sings with his whole body – lifts his head and waggles his tail with each burst of song. I know a brown thrasher is singing when he repeats each phrase of the song. You can always tell, by the distinctive song of a mourning dove to which bird you are listening. The catbird has a catlike meowing sound in its repertoire.

In the days when we had the yard full of pine siskins, we learned that their short call sounds resembled "sis", asked on a note of rising inflection. It is a long, throaty buzzing note.

Pine siskins are quite quarrelsome at the bird feeder. I watched one bully take its place on the ledge and refuse to let any of the others share the ledge, though there was room for about four of them. Each time another siskin attempted to land on the ledge, he advanced, scolding, with outstretched wing, and drove the newcomer away.

As a result, there was almost always one siskin on the feeder ledge and ten or twelve others on the ground, picking up the leftovers. Cardinals and rose-breasted grosbeaks are usually much more polite about sharing the food in the bird feeder.

You might expect that white pelicans and brown pelicans would feed in much the same way, but they have developed different methods of getting fish. Brown pelicans fly low over the water until they spot a fish, then they dive for it, usually successfully. Brown pelicans show little, if any, fear of humans. A friend of mine who is a great fisherman once befriended a brown pelican and before he knew it, the pelican was coming once a day to his porch, begging for food.

White pelicans work in a cooperative manner. In a shallow backwater of the Mississippi, called Mud Lake, a flock of white pelicans, stopping on their way south, will form a semi-circle, drawing the circle tighter and tighter until the fish are all trapped in a tight circle surrounded by white pelicans and most of them are devoured.

Avocets also have a distinctive way of getting food. They have a long, thin, curved beak. They swing this beak from side to side to find the food it stirs up from the bottom of the lake. Every year, if you' re lucky, you can watch this maneuver. Birders call one another to announce that the avocets are here. Of special interest is the way they spread their wings at times, showing the bold black and white marking on their wings.

Two fish-eating birds that are easily recognized by their actions are the anhinga and the double-breasted cormorant. The anhinga often swims with its long neck and head in view, and is sometimes called the "snake-bird" because it really does look like a snake in the water. Neither bird has waterproof wings and so each one rests on a tree limb after swimming, with its wings spread out to dry.

A bird that looks somewhat like a small duck is the pied-bill grebe. It dives for food, mostly fishes, crayfish and insects, but can stay underwater a long time and usually comes up some distance away from where it started. It is often called a "hell-diver".

Orioles have grown fond of hummingbird feeders. If, for one reason or another, the feeder is empty, the Oriole will perch on a nearby branch and scold until someone comes to refill it. To me, this is a case of flexibility, of learning to adapt to present day circumstances. I remember when I first started feeding birds, I was told to get the black oil seeds, since English sparrows did not care for them. But it took only two or three years before English sparrows adapted to the situation and learned how to enjoy the black oil sunflower seeds.

An unexpected adaptation occurred when my husband and I were eating breakfast in our Florida condo, which is on the fourth floor of a seven story building. It sounded to us as if the people in the unit above us were pounding on the floor. Since this had happened frequently of late, my husband, irritated, took a broom and tapped on our ceiling with its handle. The pounding sound stopped.

Breakfast finished, we started out on our morning walk. I heard a sound that reminded me of the pounding above our heads in the condo. I watched for several seconds and out flew a woodpecker from the metal surrounding a ventilator outlet. I suppose insects were harboring there. I pointed this out to my husband, and we had a good laugh together.

Some birds are so aggressive about their territory that we find them undesirable neighbors. Mute swans were removed from a pond a few miles from where we live because wildlife officials feared that the swans would seriously injure any child who came near them.

Other birds are aggressive when you would not expect them to be. My husband and I were sunfishing one day on Lake Belle Taine. Our attention was captured by a commotion of nearby loons. As I recall, there were eight of them, and they were obviously picking on one of them. The unwanted one would swim or fly a short distance away and then try to regain the group. We had always thought of loons as gentle creatures, whose calls we love to hear. But these loons were not gentle in their efforts to drive away the bird they must have considered an alien. They jabbed at him with their beaks, pounded on him with their wings, and voiced hostile sentiments.

At last the "foreigner" gave up and flew away. After a few seconds of hesitation another loon, probably his mate, followed him.

We still are not certain why this event occurred. Perhaps the aggressive pair had a large family (one to three young is normal), and when another pair tried to join them, they refused to let them.

A similar, but more understandable, event occurred with two gaggles of geese, each pair with goslings. One gosling got mixed up and joined the wrong family group. She was hissed at and pecked at until she returned to her own parents. An example of territorial behavior that I found disappointing was seen at Gull Lake. My granddaughter Regan had been given a bluebird house as a present, and last summer we all watched as the bluebird family moved in and successfully raised their young ones. This year, my husband and I were alone at the Gull Lake home for the weekend. I was at first delighted to see that the bluebird house was occupied. It was with disappointment that I soon discovered that the house was not occupied by bluebirds but by tree swallows. Still, it was fun to watch then as they came and went from the nest. They would often sit side by side on a limb of the tree containing the nest. Until now, my only experience with tree swallows was seeing them fly through the air at a rapid rate, catching insects in their open mouths.

To my surprise, on the third day of my watching, I saw a wren enter the house and stay there for several seconds. Was he trying to take over the nest? He came out soon, and the tree swallows returned, entered the nest, quickly came out and sat on the limb adjoining the nest. Somehow, things did not seem right. Not long afterwards we discovered two white eggs lying at the base of the tree, each one pierced by a hole made by the wren. I had heard that wrens were capable of this kind of behavior. But it was sad to see it happen.

Two weeks later, I found the bluebird house full of twigs from top to bottom. My family and I agreed that only a wren could stuff a nest that full. And soon our conclusions were proved correct, for the wren was going in and out of the house.

Birds and animals are often subject to a sense of curiosity and sometimes of playfulness. Otters especially are curious and playful. Our home in Naples adjoins a wildlife sanctuary. The sanctuary has been set aside because of a bald eagle nest and because of a rare type of tortoise. There are also bobcats to be found there and otters. Some people claim they have seen Florida panthers.

There is no question about the bobcats. A friend was working in her backyard when one bobcat chased another not far from where she was working. Before the two had gone far my friend heard the squalling noise that many animals make when mating. A few months later there were a couple of growing bobcats seen in this vicinity.

Armadillos are not playful, to my knowledge, but can become objects of play. One day a couple of playful otters took turns in reaching out with their paws and turning the armadillo on its back. The otters no doubt enjoyed this activity much more than the armadillo did.

I was playing bridge with some friends one night on the lower level of our Minnesota home. I looked up to see a creature staring in at me as if trying to help me decide what I should bid. At first I thought, "What a large cat that is, and how big and pointed its ears are." Then I realized it was not a cat but a fox. We held eye contact for perhaps half a minute before the fox turned about, flashing his red tail, which removed all doubts I had about its being a red fox.

It was probably the same red fox that my husband and I saw one night. We have a habit of turning on the backyard light before going to bed, to see if there is any activity there. We often see deer, who help themselves to the seeds in our bird feeder, refresh themselves in the bird bath, and seem to have no fear of us.

On this occasion, it was a raccoon that was in the yard, eating the seeds that had fallen from the bird feeder. She looked at us, decided we were harmless, and continued to eat. Suddenly she stiffened, became motionless, and stared at the point where the yard light drew a sharp line between illumination and the blackness of the night. Our eyes followed hers, and there, standing motionless, as if trying to size up the situation, was the red fox. His curiosity apparently satisfied, he continued on into the darkness of the night.

On another occasion the raccoon stopped eating, assumed a defensive position, and then ran into the neighboring yard. We soon saw what had chased her away. It was another raccoon, a bit smaller. He stopped to smell the sunflower seeds, then took off in the direction the other raccoon had taken. Soon we heard a squalling sound we interpreted as, perhaps, an accompaniment to mating.

Sure enough, it wasn't long before our female friend was back, this time accompanied by three young ones. Each of them had fed on the sunflower seeds that over-eager birds had spilled beneath the feeder. Mother Coon had formed the habit of jumping into the bird bath when her appetite had been satisfied. It wasn't long before the babies were copying her actions, though at the beginning they didn't always quite make it to where the water was. When the young ones were about half grown, the raccoon family left us for a more isolated area.

The most dramatic "joy of life" celebrations I have seen were those of squirrels running triangles and leaping in the air for what looked like the pure fun of it. More surprising to me was that of a young rabbit who, on a warm summer night spiced with a soft wind, was running circles near the hole in which he had been born. He was all alone, and as he jumped in the air for the pure joy of life, my heart swelled with happiness and a few of my years slipped off my shoulders.

SQUIRREL BABIES

Many people do not like squirrels, especially red squirrels, which have a reputation for being quarrelsome, and for eating bird eggs and baby birds. Many of us, however, enjoy watching the playful antics of gray squirrels, especially young ones. They become nuisances only when they start chewing on ground level wood of a house in their desire to obtain salt.

I found myself being foster parent to a couple of gray squirrel babies because of the soft-hearted qualities of my elder son, Mark, and his friend Wayne, who lived next door.

Mark and Wayne were walking back to school after lunch when they saw two infant gray squirrels on the sidewalk about to cross a busy street. It is easy to understand why they felt that if they did nothing to help, these baby squirrels would soon be squashed by the tires of a busy car or truck, as was the grown squirrel who was probably their mother.

Mark, out of breath from running, told me, "They'll be killed if we don't take care of them."

We had been having high winds the last few days. Perhaps the nest had been blown down. With no mother to care for them, the baby squirrels, desperate in their hunger, would have slim chances for survival without human help.

Most of us have been told, over and over, that it is best to leave baby animals alone, that they are not really lost or abandoned, that their mothers will return to them in time. But surely there are exceptions to this rule, as was the case here.

Funny looking little babies they were, with fur lying close to their skinny little bodies, and tails that were thin and rat-like. They were about four inches long, most unsteady on their feet. When they moved about, their back legs sprawled behind like those of a frog.

We hurried about, got a cardboard box for the new members of the family, gave them some tiny pieces of bread, which they ate with gusto, and then my husband drove the boys to school so they would be there on time.

For several days thereafter, I accomplished precious little in the way of housework. I felt that this was probably a once-in-a-lifetime experience, and I intended to make the most of it.

The boys decided it would be best to keep the squirrels together, for the sake of companionship, at our house. The offer of a neighbor to lend us a hamster cage was gratefully accepted.

All babies seem to like things warm, soft and cozy. On the very first day, the squirrels cuddled up in a piece of flannel I placed in the cage. In a few days they became quite expert at tucking themselves in. Each one would nose about until he found a nice deep fold in the cloth, then he would climb into it. Soon a paw would reach out and pull until the cloth was tucked cozily about. After a bit, you could not see a sign of squirrel, just a rumpled piece of flannel. I was reminded of a child snuggled down under the covers.

The squirrels soon decided that they preferred to sleep side by side, and on occasion I had to help the last one settle down. If he was unable to find the same fold of cloth his brother was in, he would continue to fuss. When I would lift the cloth enough so that he could climb in beside Brother, he would dart in, make a couple of circles as a dog will do before lying down, then settle happily to sleep.

Actually, we had very few problems in raising our young squirrels, but the first problem we encountered almost immediately. They were chuck-full of lice! Remembering that lice can carry quite a number of nasty diseases, I told the children, ours and all of the neighborhood children who came to observe, that they were not to touch the squirrels for the time being. I did not worry much about rabies, since this disease is almost unheard of in squirrels. Besides, these squirrels were so young they could not pierce the skin with their little teeth; yet, to be on the safe side, I did not let the children touch the squirrels during the eleven day safety period. As for the lice, I got rid of them by means of flea powder we had in the house for our Scottie. It took only two treatments; after that, there was no sign of lice whatsoever, and the treatments did not seem to affect the squirrels.

We used the trial and error method in regard to diet. Because I was quite sure these squirrels had not been weaned, I believed they might thrive best on milk. The disadvantage of giving them milk was that as soon as they'd had their fill they would start wading through the milk saucer, dragging their tails behind them. Bread soaked in lukewarm milk seemed better, for sanitary reasons. They ate this bread with such enthusiasm that you could hear smacking noises throughout the whole downstairs at feeding time. As might be expected, they growled at one another, and tried to push one another out of position near the coaster on which the food was placed. Before we gave them their freedom, we had them on a diet of nuts, water, and dry bread, which, if they stayed in our neighborhood, would be the basis of their diet.

Within twenty-four hours, these squirrels were partly tame. Instead of being terrified whenever anyone came near, they picked up their ears and looked eager when they heard voices. They already enjoyed being held, and would, at this stage, go to sleep in one's hand.

The boys named the squirrels Suki and Scooter. At first it was possible to tell them apart because Scooter was bigger. Then, as they got to be nearly the same size, I squared a bit from Suki's tail, in order to be sure of distinguishing between the two of them.

As time went by, we became aware of the differences in their personalities. Scooter, though bigger and stronger, had more fears. The first day he expressed those fears by aggressiveness. At the sight of a hand coming down into the cage, he would squeal, try his best to rear up on his hind legs and attack, claws extended. He was always more aggressive, as well as less discriminating, about his food. He would stuff himself so full that sometimes he would sit motionless, as if in a trance, for some time after eating. If petted while he was eating, he would often scold, and sometimes scratch, although he never broke a person's skin.

Suki was less interested in food, more interested in people and in play. He usually took the initiative in play, jumping upon Scooter and tumbling him over, wrestling and nibbling, and nipping him in the tail. He was more demanding about his needs. If you put him back in the cage before he'd had what he considered a fair amount of petting he would, once the gate of the cage was closed, open his mouth and emit a loud squawking sound. He discovered that this was quite a successful attention getting device, and used it every now and then, when life got a little dull.

One night Suki started squawking when it seemed to me that he really should have no complaints. I had played with him for a long time; he'd been well fed. It was dark, time, as all good squirrels know, to go to bed. Yet here he was, squawking away. So I threw another piece of flannel in the cage. He grabbed it eagerly, pulled it this way and that until it was just right for crawling under. Then he reached out and pulled it closer about him, and, making contented little sounds, settled down for a good night's sleep.

Once he'd had a taste of walnuts, Suki was quite haughty about such foods as peanuts and dry bread. The latter two items he would eat only when he was decidedly hungry.

It was amusing to watch the squirrels in their first attempt to sit up on their hind legs as adult squirrels do. Holding a piece of bread between their paws, they would sit up for a minute, topple over, try again, topple over, then resign themselves to the humiliation of having dinner in a crouching position.

Squirrels seem to have a compulsion to sharpen their teeth on anything available. Doubtful about their ability to digest wood, I removed a wooden bar on which they had been chewing, from the cage. One day I found Suki energetically chewing on a piece of metal chain which he had somehow removed from the cage door. He was as happy as a baby with a brand new teething ring. Scooter was exceedingly jealous, and kept trying to get the chain away from Suki. Suki would growl and turn his back. Try as he would, Scooter was unable to get the chain away from Suki.

We were surprised to learn that squirrels make such affectionate pets. These two used to nibble our fingers gently in play, never breaking the skin. They would roll over on their backs, and grab a finger or thumb between their paws, and pretend to nibble. They were extremely adept at clinging to a hand. Especially at night when they were tired and nearly ready for sleep, a hand thrust into their cage was an invitation for a bit of playfulness. During the daytime it was almost impossible to put your hand in the cage and withdraw it minus a squirrel. They were incredibly skillful at clinging to a hand or a wrist, or running up an arm before they could be stopped. They would stick like glue to your hand when you tried to get them back into their cage.

One day Suki escaped from a cardboard box into which I had put him and his brother while I was cleaning the cage. I saw him jump over the top, leap lightly to the floor. He scampered away, but not far. I held out my hand to him. He smelled it, and though he did not run into my hand, he offered very little resistance when I picked him up and put him back in the cage.

Only once did I get bit. That was when Suki, loose in the house, had eluded capture for several minutes. I was after him and so were my boys, and we were rather excited, because he was so skillful at slipping through our fingers. We were noisy, and I suppose he was badly frightened. I caught him just as he was climbing the stairs and he turned around and bit me.

For some days thereafter, I wore gloves when picking up the squirrels, but once they were used to having us catch them and put them back in the cage, they regarded it as a natural part of a game, and stopped biting. I gave up wearing gloves.

By now, it was obvious that they needed more exercise than they could get in their cage, yet we wanted to wait until the weather was warmer before turning them loose. We had a room off the kitchen which was used for various projects that didn't mix particularly well with good housekeeping. With a few things, such as plants, put away, it was a perfect room for giving the squirrels a romp. Two or three times a day we turned them loose in this room.

Such fun they had! Round and round the plastic straps of a chaise lounge we set up in the back room they would chase one another.

They thought the typewriter was a delightful instrument, and loved to perch on it while surveying the scene for ideas of what to do next. They would pick up a pencil in their little paws and nibble at the eraser, until I took it away from them. Scooter, who was more timid about his freedom than his brother, used to scurry back into his cage, the door of which was left open, whenever something happened to frighten him.

Climbing on us was a favorite sport. Suki used to get a certain speculative look in his eyes when he was contemplating jumping on someone. My mother, whose sense of humor was tickled by the squirrels, did not enjoy having them jump on her, and she learned to correctly interpret that gleam in Suki's eye and forestall the jump with a loud, "Oh no!" Suki, not one to force himself on anyone, would look at her somewhat reproachfully, and turn to one of the boys, or to me. He was very fond of nuzzling the boys in the ear.

One day, shortly before we decided to see if the squirrels could make it on their own, we took some pictures of them. We chose the front upstairs bedroom as the best place for the project because the light there was so good. I learned on this occasion that squirrels think African violet leaves are positively delicious.

The day finally arrived when our small pets had to be turned loose. They had been our guests for five weeks. They were strong and healthy and playful, much too active for further confinement. We'd had much discussion as to the best way to help our charges. There were five big old oak trees on our property, one of which was near the kitchen door. It had a hole it in and had once been used as a squirrel nest, but was now apparently unoccupied. Should we place some flannel in there, so that the squirrels would know it was to be their new home, and let them out of the cage at that particular spot? It seemed a good idea, except for one thing. There had once been two holes; one had now grown closed. The remaining hole was low enough so that it was easy to imagine a predator gobbling up one or both of our pets.

We finally decided to hang the hamster cage from the oak tree, in a spot where we could easily observe their progress. We hoped that, if they got into trouble, they would have sense enough to re-enter their cage. We planned to keep the cage stocked with food and water as long as they used it.

When the cage was put in place on the oak tree and the door opened, Suki took off at once, climbed up the tree a few feet, turned about to look at us, and climbed up further.

Scooter was not so sure about the value of freedom. He stayed in the cage for awhile, then jumped on top of it, sat there awhile, let us pet him, and then took off after his brother. We watched for an hour or so as they climbed about in the tree, never far apart, nibbling at leaves, jumping from branch to branch.

Needless to say, the oak tree onto which our pets had been released was observed very closely all that day. Once in a while, Scooter would come down and let us pet him. The boys busied themselves with building a little perch, or ledge, at the same height as the cage hook. Mason jar covers, holding food and water, were slipped into place at the edge of this perch.

A couple of hours after we had put the squirrels out, a very severe thunderstorm struck our area. From the security of the house to a bad storm seemed a pretty big change, so, when Scooter came to the feeding shelf during the storm, I picked him up and carried him into the house. He played happily in the room off the kitchen until the storm was over, when I turned him loose again. However, having noticed that his fur was not wet to the skin, in spite of the heavy rain, I ceased to worry about inclement weather.

Where would they sleep that night? When it was beginning to grow dark, I looked up in the tree, and in the first big crotch I saw two little tails hanging down, side by side. I have an idea this was where they spent their first night. Only once did one of them seek the security of the cage, when he was being pursued by a bigger squirrel. After a few days we took the cage down.

Grown squirrels proved to be the bane of existence for Suki and Scooter. Several times a day we would find a big squirrel chasing one of our babies round and round and round the tree trunk. A shout from us would send the big squirrels away, and bring our pets to us for protection. All of the children in the neighborhood kept a sharp eye out for the first few days. Shouts of "Get out of here!" accompanied by clapping of the hands were frequently heard. Bluejays also made life tough for our little ones. For a couple of weeks or so, the jays were able to scare the squirrels off the ledge by taking a dive at them. If we wanted to be sure the squirrels had all the peanuts they cared for, we had to stand right beside them.

It did not take too many days for our pets to get sufficiently brave to leave the "mother tree" and start exploring the woods beyond. Many times we saw the two of them wrestling and playing high in a tree. So that I could distinguish them from other squirrels at a distance I had squared their tails slightly, by clipping the fur.

In order to be accepted by other squirrels in the area, Suki and Scooter had to prove their ability to fight. Suki was the first to bear evidence of a scrap. Two days later Scooter also had a wound. It seemed rather appropriate that Scooter, the timid one, was wounded in the tail, and Suki, the bold, on the nose. After that, the scar on Suki's nose made it easy to tell the two apart.

One day when I was out in the yard, I saw Suki eating what I thought was a poisonous mushroom, and Suki knew was a very edible mushroom. I picked Suki up; he made no protest, except to more tightly clutch the piece of mushroom between his paws. I removed the offensive fungus and threw it in the garbage can. Since he had no bad effects from the part of the mushroom he had eaten, I had more respect after that for his instincts.

There was one experience I had with Suki which made me wonder if some of the behavior I had classified as aggressiveness was not, in reality, playfulness. Suki had come running across the lawn to Randy. We got peanuts and I sat down on the lawn to feed Suki. I did not want the children to feed the squirrels, now that they were running loose, because their behavior was somewhat unpredictable.

I fed Suki by hand at first, and then he jumped into my lap for each one. He sat on my knee eating away nonchalantly, but when I reached out to pet him he would scold. On one of these occasions, he turned about and grabbed my finger, without breaking my skin, but vigorously enough so that he lost his balance and ended up on his back in my lap. So what did the silly thing do? Lay there in my lap, on his back, chewing away on his peanut. What followed was even more strange. When he had satisfied his appetite to the point where, rather than eat a peanut he would bury it, he paused, gave me a speculative look, scampered about in triangular fashion, as he had in our house, ending each time with a jump into my lap. Then he would grab my fingers between his front paws, and nip them playfully, without breaking the skin.

You have probably watched a dog, when he's especially pleased with a meal, rub his whiskers on the rug or the grass, first this side, then the other side. Well, that is what Suki did now, only instead of a rug he used my skirt, which was very full, and spread out about me. Another wild circle, and he was back, tugging at the edge of my skirt, rolling over and holding it between his front paws. Another wild circle, and this time he did two somersaults in the air! I wonder how many people have seen a squirrel somersault, belly up, again and again and again, as Randy and I did that day. Suki must have played this way for fifteen or twenty minutes. Suddenly he was gone.

Suki was really quite an exceptional squirrel. He would wait for his breakfast or dinner on the feeding shelf, and, if he got hungry during the day, he would sometimes come and climb on the screen of the kitchen window, just to let remind us that he would appreciate a peanut or two.

One day, when I had fed him and he was so full he refused the last nut, he leaned over the feeding shelf as if he wanted something more. I stood close to the tree so that he could get on my shoulder. He put his cheek to mine, then turned his head and put his other cheek against mine. Before doing so, he gave me a look which said, very plainly to me, "I love you." It was a long, limpid look, characteristic not of squirrels in general, but of this one in particular.

In the days before he learned to time his visits to the feeding shelf in accordance with the hours I was apt to be in the kitchen, Suki sometimes got mighty hungry. One day I saw him hanging downward on the tree, eyes fixed on the kitchen door. When I came out, he began to make loud squawking noises, and I swear there was a reproachful quality to his voice, as if to say, "How COULD you do this to me? How COULD you let me get so hungry?"

He was so excited about the whole matter that he got the hiccups. He would take a bite of peanut, hiccup, take another bite of peanut, hiccup, and then squawk. After six or seven bites, he settled down, and everything was fine again.

Toward the end of June, our family was scheduled for a two week vacation. Naturally we worried about our pets. Wayne volunteered to put food out for them during the day. My father and mother, who lived nearby, said they would stop by in the evening. Once, when my parents arrived, they found the water dish empty and Suki, having apparently noticed where the water came from, was busily working at the end of the hose, trying to help himself. Dad refilled the water dish and gave Suki a pat on the head. Suki would eat from my father's hand, and Scooter could be patted on the head, but if the hand was brought up from behind him, he reacted defensively.

It so happened that when we drove up in front of the house, after our vacation, the squirrels were there waiting for us. Suki was apparently confused by the change in caretakers. I held out a handful of nuts for him and he would take a nut, growl, take another nut, and give another growl. The next day I saw him on the feeding shelf, and went out him. He gave me a long, hard look before taking any nuts, and I do believe that squirrel was thinking, "Oh. I remember you! " After that, things were back to normal, and he was as friendly as ever.

It was my sharp-eyed father-in-law who discovered one evening that the squirrels had built a nest for themselves in the tree which had the feeding shelf nailed to it.

There was no doubt about the fact that there was a nest up there, and that none of us had noticed it before.

"But those squirrels wouldn't build a nest!" my husband argued. "I think they are both males. Squirrels build nests for their babies. That must be an old nest we didn't notice before."

My father-in-law shook his head. "Some of those leaves are green. That's a brand new nest."

We kept watching the nest, trying to learn the truth. I confess it did not seem very logical to me that two male squirrels would build a nest for themselves, but sure enough, as we watched one night, we saw them both working away for all they were worth, adding fresh leaves to their nest.

Unfortunately, they weren't old enough or skillful enough to do a very good job of nest building. One day the boys came running into the house with the sad announcement that the nest was no longer there in the tree. When it happened, we did not know, but there had been a lot of stiff night winds, and one of them must have shaken the nest from the crotch of the tree where it was built. It fell apart in such a way that there was no sign of it except a clump of dead leaves scattered here and there beneath the tree.

Was it because of this, or because there was now a great abundance of acorns from our five oak trees that the squirrels deserted us at this point? I suspect it was because they were too busy eating and burying acorns to bother with us.

First Scooter, then Suki, began to skip a meal now and then. Scooter seemed to have a special friend, Suki had several. On August the seventeenth we left for a week at the lake. We did not worry about feeding the squirrels this time because we hadn't seen a sign of either of them for over a week. I began to remember all the funny little things about them, how they would lick the salt from their paws after eating peanuts; how Scooter once let me remove a cobweb from his whiskers, as he sat on the feeding shelf; how Suki would sometimes take a nap on the feeding shelf; how Suki used to run along the clothesline to meet me when I came with food., and how he nibbled on pencil erasers before I took them away.

They'll come back when the snow begins to fly and they get hungry, we told ourselves, but we weren't sure about that, and we actually thought it best if they were living the lives nature had intended them to live.

It was mid-September when Suki began to come around again. It took patience to get him to take food from my hand. He would play peek-a-boo around the tree with me. Sometimes he would get just an inch from the bread I was holding out, then lose nerve at the last minute. One day desire overcame fear, and he took the bread. After that, each time was easier. He was quite thin when he began coming to the house; now he was chubby again. Though his tail had grown out, he was easy to recognize, even at a distance, because he was darker than the average squirrel, especially around the mouth. The scar on his nose was barely visible.

I would never have recognized Scooter if he had not come one day with Suki and, following Suki's example, taken bread from me. But that was the last I ever saw of Scooter. Suki had bonded with me, but Scooter became a squirrel's squirrel, preferring to take his chances in the wild rather than depend on us.

As a Christmas present for birds and squirrels, we filled the empty spaces of a large pine cone with peanut butter and attached it by string to the middle of a clothesline that stretched between two of our oak trees. The birds didn't catch on right away, but the neighborhood squirrels did. They stood on their hind legs right underneath the pine cone and sniffed it yearningly. Along came Suki. It took him less than a minute to figure out how to get that peanut butter. He got on the feeding shelf, ran along the clothesline until he reached the cone, and then grabbed the cone in his mouth, propelled himself, upside down, paw after paw, pulling the cone and its string until he reached the feeding shelf. By then, half a dozen squirrels were on the feeding shelf or near it, ready to grab the peanut butter pine cone from the one who was smart enough to reach it in the first place. Although hampered by having to hang onto the cone, he managed to fight off all his competitors and disappear into the woods with his prize.

When the most bitter cold of Minnesota winter arrived, we put up a ladder under our kitchen window, so that I would not have to bundle up and walk over to the feeding shelf. Each morning I placed bread and peanuts on the top shelf of the ladder, and it did not take long before Suki learned where he could find food. Other squirrels soon learned from Suki's behavior. Before long, many squirrels climbed the ladder, and most of them looked in the window at us. They seemed as much motivated by curiosity as by hunger, for our motions inside the kitchen did not appear to cause them fear. They would sometimes sit at the top of the ladder and watch us for a minute or so before taking the food and leaving.

Suki never missed a day and seemed to consider the yard , the feeding shelf, and the ladder as his property. At sight of another squirrel near the ladder or the feeding shelf, his tail began to flick angrily. He growled and rattled his teeth, and if this didn't frighten the intruder away, he would make a dart at him. One day he was on the feeding shelf when another squirrel climbed the ladder. The other squirrel got the bread and started down the ladder. Then, because Suki was close, and growling, the intruder sat on the fourth rung, waiting. Suki jumped, landed on the fourth rung. The other squirrel fled and Suki climbed to the top and sat there awhile just to make it plain that this was HIS property.

On another occasion, Suki had taken a piece of bread from the ladder and gone to the feeding shelf with it.

A thin, mangy looking squirrel, a stranger in our neighborhood, tried to take it away from him. So far, Suki had always been successful in driving other squirrels away from the feeding shelf. But this particular squirrel refused to be intimidated. There was a brief fight on the ledge; both squirrels tumbled to the ground, then both took off to the woods, in opposite directions. After that, Suki apparently decided he had met his match. The other squirrel came quite often. Although Suki always responded by flicking his tail, growling, and darting forward, the other squirrels did not "give", and Suki did not press the issue.

Suki's possessiveness made it difficult, at first, for me to feed a scrawny looking squirrel who had lost the sight in one eye. This disabled squirrel had such a poor sense of coordination that even when I tossed a piece of bread right at him, he often missed. However, he learned to come when Suki was not around, and to announce his presence by climbing to the top of the ladder. He began to gain some much-needed weight.

By the time spring was well under way, the storm window under which I had placed the ladder for the convenience of the squirrels had been replaced by a screen. A new generation of squirrels have already located a steady source of food. They climbed the ladder and if there was no food there, they crawled all over the screen, acting indignant at finding none. Little tears in the screen appeared.

"This has gone far enough," my husband declared, and I had to admit he was right. I know that none of the squirrels needed to be fed by me. Scooter had not come to the yard for several months, and even Suki came only occasionally. So the ladder came down, and all of the squirrels in the neighborhood managed to fend for themselves.

I thought I had seen the last of our wild friends. I felt sure Suki had a nice hollow in some tree in the wooded hill that adjoined our property. After a rain, or a snowstorm, he used to appear with fur as dry as if he had been in our house. When the weather was bad, I thought of him curled up in a ball, with his bushy tail for a blanket, sleeping away the bad weather.

My last memory of Suki is a precious one. It was late summer, about a year and a half after Mark and his friend had brought the squirrel babies to our house. I had not seen him for weeks. Then one day as I was working in the yard, I saw a squirrel that reminded me of Suki. He still had the scar on his nose. He was regarding me with a steady gaze. I sat down on the lawn and called him by name. He came to me as he had once long before, and jumped in my lap. He turned over on his back, took one of my fingers between his two front paws and began to nibble ever so gently, not breaking my skin. He then jumped out of my lap, did several triangles around me, jumped in my lap again, and repeated the performance of lying on his back and taking my finger in his little paws.

I spoke gently to him as he played with me, even though I had no peanuts for him. Then he was off, scampering up a tree, as much at home in the woods as any well-adjusted squirrel should be.

INDEX

ABOUT THE AUTHOR & ARTIST

Madeline Angell has lived in Red Wing, Minnesota since marrying Kenneth Johnson in 1940; a prolific writer, she has authored five previous nature books, a biography, a history of Red Wing, a novel, and articles for magazines too numerous to list.

Marie McNamara's illustrations and designs have appeared in books, magazines, and business logos for decades. In her other life she and her husband Bruce and children Blair and Kate farm natural beef and dairy near Goodhue, Minnesota.